My UNDEAD LIFE

# My UNDEAD LIFE

## REALLY ROTTEN DRAMA

by Emma T. Graves

illustrated by Binny Boo

raintree 🌿

a Capstone company — publishers for children

Raintree is an imprint of Capstone Global Library Limited, a company
incorporated in England and Wales having its registered office at 264 Banbury
Road, Oxford, OX2 7DY – Registered company number: 6695582

www.raintree.co.uk
myorders@raintree.co.uk

Edited by Abby Huff
Designed by Brann Garvey
Originated by Capstone Global Library Ltd
Printed and bound in India

ISBN 978 1 4747 6189 5
22 21 20 19 18
10 9 8 7 6 5 4 3 2 1

British Library Cataloguing in Publication Data
A full catalogue record for this book is available from the
British Library.

# WARNING! CAUTION! BEWARE!

This story has some seriously creepy stuff. Including:

- School musical rehearsals
- A kiss. WITH MY CRUSH!!
- Stinky, rotting odours. Like, literally the worst you've ever smelled.
- Horrible friendship drama
- SMELLY SMELLS! I'm really not joking.
- Annoying little brothers
- Oh yeah, and <u>ZOMBIES</u>

Keep reading if you want, but don't say I didn't warn you.

# IT ALL ENDED WHEN . . .

I made the mistake of eating the cafeteria "food" on Mystery Meal day.

I got so sick I thought I was going to die!

When I finally stopped vomiting, I was exhausted. I slept like the dead!

And when I woke up a few things had changed.

1. I was no longer a vegetarian.

CHAPTER 1

Nobody ever said death would be easy, but I never thought it would be this *hard*. The actual dying and reanimating wasn't exactly a picnic. (So. Much. Vomiting.) But it turns out that "living" as a dead person is the really tricky bit.

Starting with looking the part.

"There!" I said, dabbing a little more concealer onto the dark circles under my eyes.

I stood back from the bathroom mirror and held out my phone. I turned my head so my friend Angela could see me from all angles through the camera lens. But she just held back a sleepy yawn on the other end of the line.

Ever since Angela worked out I was no longer among the living, she'd been helping me a lot. Her family owned the Stone Family Funeral Home. Her knowledge of caring for dead bodies came in handy. Right now we were working on my make-up skills. Except this was special make-up used on corpses.

"Well?" I asked. "How did I do?"

"You look very alive," Angela said. Then she let out another big yawn.

"Thanks. And sorry about the super early morning," I said. "I needed to make sure I had the bathroom to myself."

Now that I was dead, I didn't sleep anymore. A five o'clock beauty consultation was no problem for me. It was tougher on my new friend.

"Don't worry," Angela said. She touched the side of her nose. "Just blend right here, and you'll be good. Now, maybe I can get more sleep. See you later."

"Thanks so mu—" I started to say, but she had already hung up. Angela liked to get straight to the point.

I took another look in the mirror. My eyes were bright, and my cheeks were rosy. I didn't look like I was wearing make-up. I just looked normal. Exactly I wanted!

I was so proud of my beauty work that I considered taking a selfie and sending it to Nikki, my best friend. But I quickly pushed that thought away. Nikki didn't know I was dead. I didn't like keeping secrets from her, but that was the way things had to be.

I started tiptoeing back to my room. See, when people find out you're a member of the walking dead, they tend to pick up blunt weapons and flaming torches and come after you in giant mobs. They think you're a sign of the zombie apocalypse. They hunt you down. Even nice people, like parents, might want to bury you six-feet under so you can be "at peace".

But I still had plenty of undead life to live, and middle school was hard enough without zombie problems. So nobody could know. Just me.

Well, me and Angela.

And my little brother, Jaybee.

I passed by Jaybee's room. His door was covered in drawings of zombies and classic monster film posters. Even from the hall I could hear my brother snoring. I also caught the soft grunts of our adorable French bulldog, King Kong, who was probably curled up on Jaybee's ghoul-themed blanket.

Why would I ask for the help of a younger brother? I didn't. He had worked out what had happened to me even before I did. (Jaybee was a total horror buff, so he knew all the warning signs of the undead.) But now he was my go-to zombie expert. I had to admit, he had been pretty helpful in keeping my secret from our parents.

I made it back into my room without waking anybody up. I still had plenty of time before school. So I went to my desk, opened my laptop and started watching more online make-up videos.

I sighed as I hit play on video number thirty-one. Like I said, being a zombie was tough. There was a lot to learn. I wished I could find a video that explained how to be a living corpse. Even a pamphlet would be nice. *Anything* to make this undead life a little easier.

I glanced at the time. Soon I'd need to tackle my next challenge – breakfast.

After lumbering over to my wardrobe, I checked my outfit options. I pulled out a flowery top. A foul smell hit my nose. So I put it back and grabbed a striped shirt. I got the same weird whiff.

"Huh," I muttered to myself. "I guess I need to do some washing."

By the time I had got dressed and stumbled downstairs, Jaybee was in the kitchen. He was sitting at the worktop and wolfing down a bowl of chocolate cereal (as usual). My parents were there too, and on their phones (as usual).

"Morning, sweetie!" Mum said without looking up.

She was texting madly as she slurped a fruit smoothie. She was probably in an argument with someone, and she was probably winning. Mum was a lawyer, so winning was her job.

"Good morning, Tulah!" Dad said. He was at the cooker flipping an egg with one hand and scrolling on his phone with the other. "Ready for breakfast? As you know . . ."

"It's the most important meal of the day," Dad, Jaybee and I all said together.

Mum glanced up long enough to smile at us for teasing Dad for his predictable dadisms. The man was full of jokes, advice and terrible puns.

I sat down at the worktop. I was ready for my "most important meal". Only I wished I could just eat a bloody steak. (Raw animal protein was the only food that didn't gross me out and kept my zombie mood swings in check.) But no. Eating raw flesh would raise suspicion. Especially since I used to be vegetarian!

"Can I scramble you some eggs?" Dad asked. He raised an eyebrow. "Still on that protein diet?"

I flashed him a grin. "Yes and yes!"

I'd done my best to explain the change in my eating habits to my parents. I told them I was switching to a Paleo diet. That was where you only eat food a caveman could've had, so it basically meant a lot of protein.

But Mum and Dad weren't thrilled with me going on a diet. Now they were on my case about getting balanced nutrition. So I had to work hard to hide what I ate, and what I didn't.

"Two eggs coming up!" Dad replied.

Dad whistled as he cracked the eggs into a bowl. I cringed as he put a pan on the hob, dropped a slab of butter into it and turned on the heat.

How could I keep him from ruining my delicious raw eggs over a flame? I needed a distraction.

"Hey, Dad," I said. I pointed to the window. "Did Mr Henry get a new bike?"

"What? No way!" Dad said. He put down the bowl. Then he started feeling his pockets. "Now where did I put those glasses . . . ?"

I smiled. Dad was a mountain biker and also short-sighted. He would need his glasses to take a closer look at our neighbour's "new" ride. He walked into the living room to search for his specs.

I glanced over at Mum. She was still buried in her phone. Jaybee was watching me, but he already knew all about my raw food cravings. So I darted over to the cooker.

Now was my chance.

17

"Shh," I gestured to my brother, putting a finger to my lips. Then I turned off the heat under the pan and washed up all the dishes.

I was just about to crack one more tasty egg into my mouth, but Dad came back in with his glasses. I quickly put the egg down and backed away.

Dad peered out the window. "Ah, nope. It's still the same bike," he said. He looked at the clean, empty dishes. "Hey, did you scramble those eggs yourself?"

"Yeah," I replied. "I just couldn't wait. Growing kid and all that. Thanks, Dad. Gotta catch the bus!"

"Wait a second, Tulah," Mum said, finally setting down her phone. She looked at Dad. "Honey, I have to stay late at the office this evening. Can you pick up Tulah from rehearsal tonight?"

Dad scowled. "Uh-oh. I was going to ask you the same thing. We can't have our theatre star missing rehearsals!"

"Definitely not," I agreed. "Being in a musical is only my dream come true!"

I'd landed the lead in the Evansville Middle School autumn musical thanks to my best friend, Nikki (who tricked me into trying out). And also thanks to being a zombie (which killed my horrible stage fright). Before that, I'd spent years backstage because I was too afraid to walk out in front of an audience. Now, for the first time, I'd be able to take a bow!

"I can get a lift," I told my parents. "I know I can tag along with Nikki." My bestie was also playing a leading role in the musical.

"That'd be wonderful," Mum said. "Tell Nikki's mum we'll pick up next time."

I quickly texted Nikki. But then another thought popped into my head before I got a reply. "Oh, hey! Do you want me to make dinner for Jaybee and me tonight? Since you'll be late?"

Mum's face lit up. "Sweetie, that would be so great!"

"No problem," I said. She didn't need to know it would be great for me too. I'd get to avoid another awkward family meal *and* eat whatever I wanted.

Mum stood up and planted a kiss on my forehead. But then she pulled back. Her nose wrinkled up.

"And Jaybee, maybe you could take the rubbish out," Mum said. "Something smells nasty in here."

"*Mmm-hmm-fmm*," Jaybee mumbled through his full mouth.

I sniffed the air. Something did smell. It was a familiar scent too. I looked around for King. Maybe he needed a bath?

Then my eyes grew wide as I realized – it was the same stench from my clothes! I quickly backed out of the kitchen and hurried to the bathroom.

I closed the door. I took a whiff of my armpit.

*Ugh.* It smelled a little bit like deodorant and a lot like dirty socks boiled with cabbage. Then I smelled my arm.

It smelled like a turkey sandwich. A really, REALLY old turkey and cheese sandwich that had been left out in the sun and had grown three kinds of mould. I put a hand in front of my mouth.

"*Haah,*" I breathed. I sniffed.

I gasped and then slapped a hand over my mouth to keep my eggs down.

The smell coming from my insides was like curdled milk and rotten meat wrapped in the stinkiest cheese on Earth.

I steadied myself on the worktop and looked into the mirror. Jaybee could take out the kitchen bin every hour on the hour, but it wasn't going to fix the stink.

The nasty stench was all me!

# CHAPTER 2

I brushed my teeth again before rushing out the door. There was nothing else I could do without missing the bus. I just hoped nobody would notice my stinky odour.

Nikki was already at the stop when I shuffled around the corner. I waved. She looked right at me and then looked away.

*Weird*, I thought. I checked my phone. Nikki hadn't texted back about getting a lift after rehearsal. *Double weird.*

I walked over as fast as I could with stiff knees. *Rigor mortis* was a serious pain. That's when dead muscles become stiff. It didn't actually hurt (nothing did anymore), but it did make me clumsy and slow.

The bus was pulling up when I finally

reached the stop. "Hey, did you get my text?" I asked Nikki as I followed her up the stairs.

Nikki didn't say a word. She kept walking and sat down next to Carla Rivas.

"Uh. Nik, there's a seat down there." I pointed to an empty spot where we could both sit, like we *always* did.

Nikki didn't even look up. "I guess you'd better go and grab it," she said.

*Whoa.* I stood still, even though I was holding up the queue. *What is happening?*

"Let's go," the kid behind me grumbled.

I didn't move. "Nikki, what's wrong? Are you mad at me?"

"Better hurry so you can save that spot for *Angela*," Nikki replied in a snotty voice.

I was stunned. I'd heard her use that voice before. Nikki used it on know-it-all Bella Gulosi when she started acting like the teacher. She had used it on Kenneth Norberg that time he said girls couldn't pitch. But she had never used it on me.

"Take a seat!" Gus, the bus driver, shouted.

Those were the only three words Gus ever spoke. If I didn't do as he said, he would shout them again, only louder.

Then Bella, my least favourite person in the world, joined the chorus of grumblers. "Seriously, Tulah. Can you get a move on before we all die from old age?"

I looked at Nikki. I waited for her to use the snotty voice on Bella. I waited for her to say this was all a joke, or to even look at me. She just stared straight ahead.

"Any day now!" somebody further back in the queue shouted.

"I didn't know everybody was so anxious to get to school," I mumbled. Couldn't they see my best friend was upset? Didn't they understand I was having a crisis?

I walked on and slumped into the empty seat – by myself. *What did I do?* I wondered. *Why was Nikki talking about Angela? Why is Nikki so mad? We were fine on Friday. At least I thought we were.*

But then I started thinking back . . .

25

I sank further into my bus seat. OK, so maybe I hadn't been hanging out with Nikki lately. Maybe I had been doing more stuff with Angela instead. But Nikki had to know she was, and always would be, my best friend!

At the last stop Angela got on. She slid in to the seat across from me. She was dressed all in black, as usual. And, as usual, she didn't say very much.

"What's with . . . ?" She lifted her chin towards Nikki.

"I think she's mad," I said softly. "I've just been spending a lot of time dealing with my, uh, issues."

Angela nodded. I didn't have to explain my issues to her.

That reminded me. . . .

I held my hand out across the aisle. "Do I smell fresh to you?"

Angela looked at me funny and then leaned in for a sniff. She immediately drew back and pressed a hand over her mouth.

"Oh. *Ulp.* You're not exactly . . . *daisy* fresh," she choked out. It looked like she was trying not to vomit. "I was wondering when this would start."

I stared at her. "When *what* would start?"

"I think you're beginning to . . . decay," Angela whispered.

"Decay? *Noooooo!*" I moaned softly. I let my big, fat rotting head drop into my hands.

Make-up was great for hiding my dead outside. It could cover up greying skin. It could even patch up cuts and scrapes that would never heal. But I was going to have to do something about my rotting *insides* before I smelled more disgusting than the dumpster behind Frank's Diner!

Soon the bus pulled up in front of the school. I was still coming to terms with this new problem.

"Don't worry," Angela said, dragging me from my seat. "It'll be fine."

As I got off the bus, I spotted Nikki's blond head darting through the crowd. How could

27

I have already forgotten about my other new problem? I had to straighten things out with Nikki right away.

"Nikki!" I called out.

Angela stepped onto the pavement and stood next to me. "We'll think of something to stop your rotting guts," she finished.

That's when Nikki turned. She saw Angela whispering in my ear. She scowled, quickly turned back and disappeared into the mass of kids.

I sighed and walked with Angela up the school steps. I hoped I could find a solution soon, to both issues. At the moment I wasn't sure which was worse – smelling like a pile of rubbish or being ignored by my best friend.

By the time I made it to the lockers, Nikki had already gone. In our first lesson she made sure she sat in a spot where there weren't any more free seats. It seemed like she was determined to avoid me.

*Maybe it's a good thing,* I tried to tell myself as I slumped in a chair on the other side of the room.

After all, I couldn't have her or anyone else working out that I had passed my expiration date. If the people around me started to realize that the smell of dead fish was coming off *me,* I'd be in real trouble. It was best to keep my distance. From everyone.

So I sat at the back in all my lessons.

"*Phew!* Does anyone else smell liverwurst and pickled garlic?" Mr Stein asked during algebra. I shrunk down in my seat.

During PE I hid in the changing room.

At lunch I went to the library. It was my favourite spot for lunch ever since I'd got the zombie virus from the cafeteria food. The librarian started sniffing the moment I stepped inside. I ducked behind the shelves until she turned on a fan.

"Sorry," I whispered to Angela as I sat down at our table in biology.

My unlucky lab partner just scrunched up her nose and nodded. I think she was holding her breath.

All day I tried to keep my stink to myself. And all day one question played over and over in my head. *What am I going to do about rehearsal?*

The *Musical High* rehearsals had been going on for almost two weeks. They were the highlight of my undead life. My zombie nerves of steel had helped me land the lead. But I feared my zombie stench of death was about to get me kicked off the stage!

When the last bell rang, I dragged myself to the hall – literally. My trainers squeaked on the hall floor as I lugged them closer, step by step.

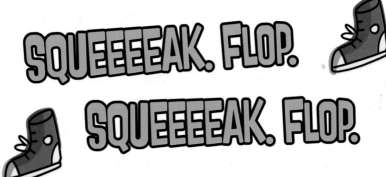

SQUEEEEAK. FLOP. SQUEEEEAK. FLOP.

I paused in front of the hall's double doors to pull on my coat. It wasn't chilly, but I zipped it all the way up to my neck. Maybe it would hold in any odours.

"Tulah?" Mr Hammer, the director, called as soon as I walked in. "We need you onstage!"

I tried to stay positive as I lurched over. I was grateful that we were just running blocking. Working out where everybody had to be onstage was easy. At least it wasn't choreography, which I struggled to pull off on my stiff legs. But I was less grateful when Mr Hammer called the next name.

"Jeremy?" he said. "Let's get you up here too. We'll pick up where we left off last Friday, when Todd and Isabella meet."

I watched as Jeremy Romero bounded towards the stage. Jeremy had only been going to Evansville for a couple months. That was just long enough for me to fall madly-in-like with him. I had been too shy to do anything about my secret crush.

But when Jeremy and I auditioned, something amazing happened. Thanks to my zombie bravery, I didn't go brain-dead the way I usually did around cuteness. During the past two weeks of rehearsals, I'd been practically normal around Jeremy.

But now? I didn't want him to come within fifty feet of me!

Jeremy took the stairs two at a time. He bounced to a stop onstage next to me.

"Hey," he said.

Then Jeremy flashed a smile. That totally adorable grin had landed him the role of Todd, the main guy of *Musical High*. He was the love interest to my character, Isabella.

I gave a small smile but kept my lips tightly sealed and took a step back. I wasn't about to let a gust of my nasty breath hit Jeremy's face.

So how was I supposed to pull off this cute scene where our characters first meet? All that happened was our hands accidentally brush as we talk, and we both get embarrassed.

Then the scene ended in a song. . . . OMG.
I was going to have to sing right to him!

"You OK, Tulah?" Jeremy asked.

I nodded. "I think I'm getting a cold,"
I mumbled. I put my hand over my mouth
and took another step back. "I just don't
want it to spread."

Mr Hammer started shouting directions
and writing everything down in his big red
binder. The progress was slow.

"Tulah, stand stage left!" he shouted.
"Face front!"

Luckily our director was so focused on
working out the blocking that he didn't
notice me acting weirdly.

Nikki did. She was sitting in the front
row, waiting for her cue. And glaring. Her
character, Poodle, had the funniest lines
in the musical. But Nikki didn't look very
happy now.

I searched the wings for Angela while
Mr Hammer worked on Jeremy's/Todd's
entrance. Angela was the stage manager

and handled a lot of the backstage stuff.
I hoped to spy a friendly face in the dark.
All I saw were shadows.

"OK, kids! From the top of the song!"
Mr Hammer called.

The music began to play, and Jeremy
launched into our first duet. He took a step
towards me. I stepped back. He stepped
closer. I stepped back.

"Perfect!" Mr Hammer yelled. "Now
let him catch up to you, Tulah. Then sit
together on the bench."

I couldn't sit next to Jeremy in my stinky
state! I ran a few steps away and pretended
to have a sneezing fit.

"Sorry," I said, keeping my hands over
my mouth. I pretended to let out another
sneeze.

Mr Hammer frowned. "I hope you're not
coming down with something, Tulah," he
said. He sighed. "All right, let's wrap things
up early."

My cold act worked! If I wasn't so worried about my foul mouth, I would've let out a huge sigh of relief. But before we could get off the stage, Mr Hammer waved Jeremy and me over.

"Just a heads up, you two," Mr Hammer said. "Tomorrow we're going to start including the kiss in rehearsals."

I gulped and then coughed and covered my mouth again. *We're doing the kiss?* I thought. *Tomorrow? So soon?*

I must have looked panicked. Because when Jeremy glanced over, he smiled a little. "It won't be *that* bad," he said.

*OMG!* I screamed in my mind. *He thinks I don't want to kiss him!*

"No," I choked out. "It's not that at all. It's just – I don't—"

Mr Hammer interrupted my spluttering. "The kiss is nothing to stress over. We have a few weeks to make sure it isn't awkward before we open. It's just a stage kiss!"

*Just a stage kiss.* I let out a small laugh.

Opening my mouth was a mistake.
Mr Hammer wrinkled his nose. "Can you guys smell something?"

Jeremy looked around. "What *is* that? Skunk?"

I shrugged and backed up towards the stairs. I had to get away before they realized *I* was what reeked.

I had always known the kiss was coming. It was going to be awkward no matter how you sliced it. After all, I hadn't ever kissed anyone besides my mum, my dad and my dog.

But awkward was the least of my worries. If Jeremy discovered I was the source of the lethal stench, it would be *my* kiss of death.

CHAPTER 3

I hurried off the stage, grabbed my backpack and headed for the exit as fast as I could. All I wanted was to get home.

But as I pushed through the front doors, I remembered *how* I was supposed to get home. I stopped dead in my tracks.

"*Uuuugggghhh!*" I moaned. I had told my parents I could get a lift with Nikki and her mum!

I felt awful. I smelled worse. I was in no shape to face my former best friend – the one who had been avoiding me all day!

I took out my phone and scrolled through my contacts. I desperately searched for somebody else I could call for a lift.

But Lacey DuChamp had football. I hadn't seen Angela at rehearsal. There was no one.

I let out a long sigh and continued towards the road.

Nikki was already waiting there. I shuffled over slowly. I came to a stop by her side and stood silently.

I didn't know what to say. How could I explain that I wasn't trying to ignore her without telling her everything (which would ruin everything)?

"Hey," is all I managed to come up with.

Nikki looked at me but didn't respond. Her eyes were cold.

"Can I get a lift home?" I asked. "My parents are working late."

Nikki just shrugged. That probably meant no, but at the same moment her mum pulled up.

"Hi, Tulah!" Nikki's mum shouted out the window. "Do you need a lift?"

I was saved. Oh, and also doomed.

As soon as I got inside my house, I went straight up to the bathroom. I filled the bath with Sweet Strawberry Bubble Bath and jumped in. But it was no use. The smell was coming from my guts. No amount of scrubbing could get rid of it.

So I did what any desperate zombie would do.

I pounded on Jaybee's door. You know things are bad when you need the advice of a nine-year-old.

"Come in!" he called.

I opened the door. Jaybee was sprawled on his bed. His backpack full of homework was zipped tight, and he was nose-deep in his favourite comic, *Zombie Boy Z*.

King Kong was lounging on the bed too. When I came in, he immediately jumped down and waddled over. He began sniffing all around my feet.

"So, I've got a . . . problem," I started. I stayed on the far side of the room. It didn't help.

"So I smell," Jaybee said, coughing and squishing up his face. "Are you – *HACK!* – rotting – *COUGH!*"

"Yes," I moaned. "I'm dead meat."

Jaybee blinked. I think my stench was making his eyes burn. "Right. I never thought about what would happen to your insides. After all, you can't smell the zombies in comics." He held his nose and made fanning motions. "But maybe that's a good thing!"

I rolled my eyes as he burst out laughing. Not helpful.

"Seriously, Jaybee. What am I going to do?" I asked when he finally stopped. "I can't go walking around smelling like roadkill! Someone will eventually work out that *I'm* what stinks. Which will lead to questions. Which will lead to discovering I'm a zombie."

Jaybee went quiet. He kept one hand firmly pinched over his nose. "What about deodorant? They say Sword Body Spray cuts through any odour," he suggested, quoting the tagline. "Oh, and maybe gum? Mint-a-Stick keeps you fresh all day!"

"You watch too many adverts," I told him.

But I'd seen the ads too. If their big claims were true, it might actually work.

"I guess it's worth a shot," I admitted. "Thanks."

"No problem," Jaybee said. He waved his free hand. "Now get out of here. You're smelling up my space! And don't worry about dinner. I'll get my own. I don't want you to foul up my food."

"Thanks," I said again, and I meant it. I could use the extra time to set my plan into motion.

I went back to my room, and King happily trotted behind. He was probably the only one who enjoyed my new stinky smell.

I searched through my desk, looking for money. With last week's allowance, I had about twenty-four dollars. I shoved the cash into my pocket and checked the time. It was 6.12 p.m. My parents could be home as early as 7.00 p.m.

I looked down at the furball by my feet. "Want to go for a walk?"

King Kong's tail wagged as if it were about to fly off his behind. He sniffed my ankles all the away down the stairs.

For supper I quickly gulped down some raw eggs and gave King a scoop of dog food. Then I clipped on his lead.

"I'm walking King to the chemist!" I yelled up to Jaybee. "Make sure you've finished dinner before seven. And wash up afterwards!"

"Or what? You'll eat my brains?" Jaybee shouted back.

"Ha, ha," I muttered as I stepped out of the front door.

It was about a mile to the chemist. King

Kong and I made it in no time, even with all King's pit stops and my lurching walk. I tied him up in front of the shop.

"Be right back," I promised.

Inside, I filled my basket. The cashier gave me an odd look when I dumped five cans of Sword Body Spray and about twenty packs of Mint-a-Stick onto the counter.

"Will that be all?" the cashier asked.

I nodded and handed over my money. I certainly hoped this would be all. I was now completely broke until Sunday.

When I stepped outside, I opened a pack of gum and popped a piece into my mouth. I could instantly taste the freshness as I began to chew.

I breathed in to my hand. A wave of minty air hit my nose.

*Yes!* I thought. *Thank you, Mint-a-Stick!* Finally I could breathe that sigh of relief – without worrying about making anyone sick. I hoped the body spray would work just as well.

I checked my phone. It was 6.37. That would be plenty of time to get back home before my parents.

As I bent down to untie King, he jumped up and started licking my face.

I laughed. "Thanks, buddy."

Sure, King Kong was a dog, and he rolled in things that smelled like rotting zombie flesh for fun. But at least King liked kissing the new, mintier me.

*Maybe Jeremy won't mind kissing me either,* I hoped.

# CHAPTER 4

"Let's go!" Mum yelled up the stairs the next morning. "You're going to be late if we don't leave soon."

"Coming!" I shouted from my room.

I blasted myself one more time with Sword Body Spray. Then I popped in another piece of gum, grabbed my backpack and headed to the car. Jaybee was already sitting in the back when I slid in.

I think Mum felt bad about getting home late the night before. So to make up for it, today she was driving Jaybee and me to school. I was more than happy to take her up on it. The journey to school took half as long in a car – and I didn't have to worry about sitting alone on the bus.

"Whoa!" Mum said as she climbed in the front. She fanned her face.

*Uh-oh,* I thought, gripping my backpack. *Was the spray not strong enough?*

"Jaybee, is that smell coming off of you?" Mum asked. "You know you're too young for aftershave."

Jaybee shot me a dirty look.

"Sorry!" I mouthed to my brother. But I was secretly happy all Mum was smelling was the body spray, and that the only one she was blaming was Jaybee.

"It was just a sample I got," Jaybee lied to Mum, still glaring at me. "I wanted to try it."

Mum rolled down her window and then pulled out of the driveway. "Well, hopefully it'll wear off soon," she said.

*Hopefully not!* I silently pleaded.

The body spray was still working its magic during my first lesson.

Phew!

Whoa, who set off the perfume bomb?

And the gum was working too.

CHOMP
CHOMP
CHOMP

Maybe too well . . .

POP!

48

49

I'd spent time in the head teacher's office before, but that was for student government. I'd never been *sent* to her office.

I should've been freaking out. I should've been worrying that Ms Moody would call my parents, or that I would be kicked out of the musical. I was definitely freaking out. But not about any of that.

I stared at the tooth in my hand. My tooth, my *permanent* tooth, had come out. What would I lose next? My head?

"Tulah Jones, I'm surprised," Ms Moody said as she walked in.

I quickly shoved the loose tooth into my pocket.

Moody wrinkled her nose and opened the window behind her desk before taking a seat. She waved her hand at the massive pile of gum packs on her desk and said, "I know you know the rules about gum in school."

I nodded. Of course I did. One of the first jobs student government had was holding an assembly to tell everyone the school rules.

We each had to speak a rule into the mic. "No gum or sweets" was rule number three, my rule. Addressing the entire school had been so terrifying that the gum rule would be burned into my memory forever.

"This behaviour simply isn't like you. I expect more from you, Tulah," Moody went on in that disappointed voice adults use.

"Yes, Ms Moody," I replied seriously. But inside I was trying not to laugh. She expected more from me. But with pieces of me falling off, soon there might be a lot *less*.

"I should give you afterschool detention," Moody explained. "But it wouldn't be fair to punish the rest of the kids in the musical by keeping you from practice. So instead, let's call this during-school detention."

She paused to choke out a cough. "Plus, with all that perfume, it may be best that you stay in here," she added. "Just, uh . . . keep the window open." With that, she swept all my precious gum into her rubbish bin.

I gulped. I wished I could be sent home.

"Between the two of us, you don't need to wear so much perfume," Ms Moody said, softening slightly. "Some pupils might be allergic to it. And if you practise good hygiene, it's unnecessary."

I nodded. Moody had no idea.

"Oh, and I'll be taking your phone too." She held out her palm.

I reluctantly handed it over. Any hopes of texting Angela or searching for videos on how to reattach a tooth were gone.

Moody walked out. She took my phone and the bin of minty freshness with her.

As soon as the door clicked shut, I took my homework out of my backpack. I thought I could use the distraction. It turned out I was distracted enough.

I worked through the same maths problem three times. I wore a hole in my science worksheet after answering and then erasing the same question over and over. Don't even ask me about English – I was no longer sure if it was my first language.

I put down my pencil. I was worried about what parts of me I would lose next. It didn't matter how fresh I smelled if I couldn't work out a permanent solution to my rotting problem.

And I worried that Nikki was never going to speak to me again. I turned the glittery pencil in my hand. It was one that Nikki had lent me. More than anything I wanted to spill my guts to her.

No, scratch that. Spilling my guts was not what I wanted to do! I just wanted to talk to my best friend.

Finally, the last bell sounded. I shoved everything into my bag and stood up. Ms Moody opened the door before I had both arms through the straps.

"All right, Tulah. I hope you've learned your lesson," Moody said. Then she sniffed. "It also seems your perfume has worn off enough that it won't be a hazard to other pupils. Now, off you go to rehearsals."

Moody handed me my phone, and I started for the door. She sniffed again.

"Was it tuna casserole day in the cafeteria?" she asked.

"Uh, yeah. I think," I mumbled as I rushed out of her office.

*Or has my spray just worn off TOO much?* I wondered.

It didn't matter. Without the gum, I was doomed. I could practically taste the rotten fumes building up inside of me. There wasn't a person in the world who would want to pucker up for me.

I headed towards the hall anyway. Old Tulah (the live version) would have been in tears as she walked through the corridors. Or she would have run screaming out of the building.

And why not? I was living a complete nightmare.

1. My best friend wasn't speaking to me.

2. I was in trouble at school.

3. I was about to kiss Jeremy Romero on a stage, in front of a group of people, with death breath and DBO (dead body odour).

But new, post-life Tulah just marched towards her unhappy ending. It was weird. It was almost like I couldn't stop.

Jaybee had explained to me that in all the films and comics, zombies didn't usually have feelings – just impulses. They lumbered on no matter what. Traps, fires, bullets . . . nothing slowed them down. Zombies just kept going.

Speaking as a real-life zombie, the idea that we had zero feelings didn't seem right. I couldn't feel pain, physically. But I still felt sad and embarrassed and frustrated. It was only my reactions to those feelings that had changed. I didn't get sick or freeze up or pass out when I was sad or scared. I just kept going.

I half laughed, half grunted as I stepped into the hall.

Old Tulah would have been falling apart *emotionally* over all this.

But new Tulah? I slid a hand into my pocket. I closed my fist around my molar. New Tulah was straight-up falling apart.

## CHAPTER 5

"Where are you, Angela?" I whispered.

I squinted into the darkness from the last row of seats in the hall. Angela was probably backstage ordering people around.

Being stage manager was a big job. You had to make sure everything went smoothly, and you had to be ready to solve any crisis that might pop up. Plus it all happened behind the scenes, in the dark – which was just the way Angela liked it.

I hoped Angela was ready to handle another emergency. I took out my phone.

**ME:** *Help!*

I sent the text and waited. Angela would know what to do.

**ME:** *I'm falling apart! My tooth came out in class.*

I tapped my foot. Angela *had* to know what to do.

**ME:** *They took all my gum. Me = death breath.*

I tapped my other foot. Onstage Mr Hammer was finishing up with the scene before *the scene.* I was running out of time.

**ME:** *The kiss is today! WHAT AM I GOING TO DO? HELP!!!*

"Jeremy? Tulah? Let's go! Come to the stage!" Mr Hammer called.

My time was up. I took a final look at my phone. Nothing from Angela.

I was on my own.

If I still had a pulse, my heart would've been pounding as I made my way to the stage. But it wasn't. I only had a deep, deep sense of dread. The kind that makes you want to cling to your best friend.

I walked past Nikki on my way up. She was sitting in the front row. But when I glanced over, she quickly pretended to be studying her script.

"Are you two ready?" Mr Hammer asked when Jeremy and I were both onstage. "Remember, your characters haven't been together since their summer fling. But you haven't been able to stop thinking about each other."

Jeremy nodded. His cheeks were red, and he kept looking at his shoes. I couldn't move. Then Jeremy took a deep breath and looked up long enough to flash me a knee-weakening smile.

"Today's the day," Jeremy said.

*Yeah,* I thought. I tried to smile. *Today's the day my undead life ends. Today is the day my death breath gives away my secret.*

"Whenever you're ready," Mr Hammer told us.

Isabella, what are you doing here?

Todd. I was going to ask you the same thing.

Speak up, Tulah! Not so stiff!

There was nothing I could do except say my lines and try to keep my distance.

We just moved in.

I can't believe it. We're neighbours! I-I thought I'd never see you again!

I've been thinking about you since last summer. There's something I wanted to give you . . .

Oh? What?

There was no escape!

60

Angela dragged me off the stage.

"That was close," I mumbled. Then I noticed Angela was walking right past the dressing rooms. "Wait, I thought—"

"I got your texts. It sounded like an emergency to me," Angela replied. "Maybe not a *costume* related one, but . . . I did what I had to do."

I grinned. Angela Stone, the dark cloud of Evansville Middle School, was my silver lining! She had made up a story just so I wouldn't have to kiss Jeremy and blow my cover. I almost couldn't believe it.

Once we were in an empty back corridor, Angela steered me around a corner. Then she stopped and turned around.

"OK. Now tell me what's going on," Angela said.

"I'm coming apart!" I dug my tooth out of my pocket and showed it to her. "This popped out when I was chewing gum. Who knows what I might lose next?"

Angela stared at it. "*Hmmm.*"

"Well? Is there any way we can stick it back in?" I was leaning close when I whispered the last part, and Angela immediately jerked back. "*Ugh!* And I still smell like a rubbish dump in July."

I leaned against the wall. "What will I do? Am I going to turn into a giant lump of muck?"

"Wait here," Angela said. "I have an idea. I just need to get something out of my locker."

She slipped away without another word. I sighed and slid down the wall until I was sitting on the floor. I let my head fall onto my knees. What kind of social life could I have if I couldn't keep myself together? I felt like things could not get any worse.

So of course they did.

"TULAH JONES!" a voice yelled. "I have had it!"

Nikki came flying around the corner in a rage. I whipped my head up so fast it hit the wall behind me.

**TUNK!**

It should have hurt, but it didn't. What hurt was the look on Nikki's face.

She was so mad her face was red. Her hands were balled into fists. Apparently she was also speaking to me again. Or at least she was yelling at me.

"You're acting like a totally different person!" Nikki screamed. "Sneaking around! Avoiding lunch! Now this! There wasn't any costume emergency. You're just running off with Angela Stone again. What is wrong with you?"

"I-I . . . ," I stammered helplessly.

In my head I was telling her everything. *I'm sorry, Nikki. The truth is, I'm a zombie. I've been dead for weeks. Remember that cafeteria sludge I ate? Well, it killed me. Now I'm literally falling apart and Angela's helping me, but what I could really use is my BFF.*

But if I told her the truth, we would *never* be friends again. I knew it. Who wants to be BFFs with a pile of rotting flesh?

"Say something! What is wrong with you?" Nikki repeated, planting her fists on her hips.

*Everything*, I thought.

"Nothing," I lied. "Nothing is wrong."

"*Nothing?*" Nikki said. "You've been acting weird ever since you got the lead in the musical! Are you too good for me now? Or maybe you just don't need me anymore? Is that why you're always hanging out with – with *Morticia*?"

"No! Nikki, you're my best friend. I just . . ." I trailed off. Then Angela poked her head around the corner.

"Hey, you guys!" she said. Angela smiled at us. Nikki glared at her. "Rehearsal just ended, so we're finally free to go home!"

Nikki kept glaring. Angela kept smiling. She was completely oblivious. "So, Tulah, do you want to come over to my house? We can finish that, uh, biology homework. . . . I think I have a solution for that problem you were struggling with." Angela raised an eyebrow.

"Yes!" I agreed quickly. Too quickly.

I glanced over at Nikki. She still looked angry, but now her eyes were watery. She thought I was choosing Angela over her!

"Nikki, I—" I started. But I couldn't seem to form complete sentences. "Do you . . . ?"

"Go!" she snarled at me. "Go and hang out with your new best friend. Don't worry about me."

Nikki turned and stomped off. Angela gave me a questioning look, but I didn't know what to say. So I just stood up and started walking.

Honestly, I *was* worried. About a lot of things. But especially about Nikki.

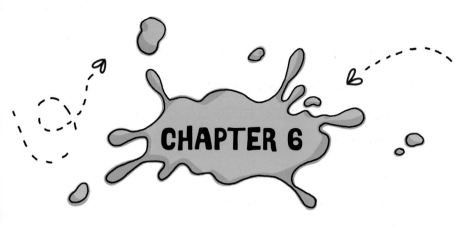

# CHAPTER 6

"Have you thought about telling her?" Angela finally asked, breaking the silence as we walked to her house.

"Yes," I said. "And I've also thought about how Nikki will run away screaming. Not everyone is as comfortable with the undead as you are."

"True," Angela agreed.

I followed her up a walkway, through an arched trellis and onto the porch of Stone Family Funeral Home. Or as Angela called it, "home".

Angela pushed open the front door. Suddenly I was face-to-face with half a dozen empty coffins. They were on display in the room. All of them were open wide.

It almost felt like the coffins knew I was dead and were inviting me to climb inside. It was more than a little creepy.

"This way," Angela said. She led me through the coffin showroom, to a door and down a set of stairs.

The basement was even spookier than the coffin room. It looked like the morgues you see in hospital and crime TV series. Only this was smaller. Two metal tables stood in the centre, and cabinets filled with mysterious liquids lined the walls.

Beside the tables were what looked like tool chests on wheels. A few shiny tools sat on top. They looked like they could belong to a make-up artist or a surgeon . . . or both.

"We prep the bodies down here. This is where the magic happens!" Angela said, beaming.

Old Tulah would have needed to lie down at this point. Luckily new Tulah just stood there. It was a lot to take in.

"What are those?" I asked finally. I pointed to a couple of handles on the wall.

"Refrigerator drawers," Angela said. "We store bodies in there. If we could just keep your body chilled, it wouldn't be breaking down so fast. But we can't keep you in a freezer. Not if you want to try to live your normal life."

"Maybe I should move to Antarctica," I grumbled. "But I guess that wouldn't exactly be living my normal life either."

"OK!" Angela clapped her hands together, ignoring my doom and gloom. "First, let's fix your tooth."

She started digging around in one of the drawers on the tool chest. I think I heard her humming. I swear she was enjoying herself. She pulled out a small tin full of strange putty, a tiny drill and some things that looked like screws.

"Soft tissue is the first part of you that will decay," Angela said.

She said it like it was no big deal. Like the "soft tissue" wasn't my actual flesh. Like "soft tissue" wasn't my *face*.

"You mean my nose is going to fall off?" I whimpered. I reached up and held onto my nose. I wanted it to stay right where it was.

Angela looked up from whatever she was doing to my tooth. She finally seemed to realize I was flipping out.

"Don't worry," she said. "I have an idea for the soft stuff. And the good news is, your bones and teeth should stay strong for a long time. Let's just get this one back where it goes."

Angela held up my tooth. It now had a tiny metal post on it. "Lie down," she said, gesturing to the long metal table.

"Where the corpses usually lie?" I asked. "Just great."

I climbed on. I tried to relax and tried not to think about all the other dead bodies that had been on this slab.

"Drink up!" Angela said, handing me the mysterious blended beverage. "The recipe may need tweaking. I was winging it. But the ingredients should really help."

I took a sip. "Not bad," I said. "It's not trying to come right back up, like cooked food does. So that's a plus. What's in it?"

"Embalming fluid. Formaldehyde mostly, like what Ms Rogi used on the frogs we cut up in biology. Embalming fluid would kill a living body, but it keeps dead bodies from breaking down and getting stinky," Angela explained.

That sounded good to me. I glugged down some more.

"I also put in a couple of raw eggs, because I don't want you getting hungry for brains," Angela joked. "I've got a good head on my shoulders, and I'd like to keep it!"

*SNUURRF!* I snorted, because that was funny and because the idea of me eating brains was terrifying. The embalming smoothie dribbled out of my nose.

"Huh, it smells a little like pickles," I said, dabbing away the liquid. Then I sighed. "Which means *I'm* probably going to smell a little like pickles."

Angela shrugged. "Yeah, it's weird, but it beats stinking like roadkill," she said. "You should probably drink this stuff once a day. Maybe even twice. I'll give you the recipe so you can make it at home."

She bent over a piece of paper and made some notes. Then she started loading bottles into a box.

"My family orders loads of embalming fluid every week," Angela explained. "It shouldn't be too hard to sneak you the ingredients. This will be enough to get you started."

I was sucking down the last of my smoothie when we heard a car pull up to the house. Angela shoved the box into my hands and started cleaning up *fast*.

"That's my parents!" she said. "I'm not supposed to be down here without my dad."

I stared down at the box of ingredients. "Angela, how can I ever thank you for all—"

"Later," she said, pushing me up the stairs with the blender under her arm. "We have to get out of here now, or you won't be the only dead kid in Evansville!"

# CHAPTER 7

"Wow! What's all that?" Dad asked when he picked me up at Angela's.

"It's for a science project I'm working on with Angela," I lied. I slid the big box of ingredients into the back seat of the car.

"Ooh, fun! What kind of project are you doing?" he asked, reaching for the lid.

I put my hand out to stop him. "Sorry. It's top secret."

Dad fake pouted and climbed in the front while I made a mental note to get started on a science project. I got in the car next to my box of corpse juice.

I started to lower the window for stench control. But then I took my finger off the button.

*I don't have to!* I realized. I took a quick sniff to double-check. The foul cloud had finally lifted! Angela's embalming smoothie was working already.

I leaned back and closed my eyes for the short ride home. It was nice not smelling like a dirty nappy on a hot day. But the magic stink-stopping juice couldn't fix all my problems. I still had all the grace of Dorothy's Tin Man (pre-oilcan), a craving for raw meat and a best friend who wasn't speaking to me.

When we got home, I told my parents that I'd eaten at Angela's (which was technically true) and needed to work on my project. Before they could insist I sit through a hot cooked meal, I shut myself in my room.

I crawled into bed, but I didn't sleep. I stared at the ceiling the whole night, and not just because of the no-sleep-for-the-dead thing. I was thinking about Nikki.

Tulah and Nikki.

Nikki and Tulah.

The two of us just went together. We had been best friends since we met on the carpet in kindergarten. From that first sharing circle until now, I had always told Nikki *everything*.

I got why she was mad. She sensed I was keeping things from her. She saw me hanging out with Angela, someone new, for no obvious reason. How was she supposed to know it was a life or death-breath situation making me act so weird?

I picked up my phone and started to text.

**ME:** *Nik, I'm sorry I—*

I deleted everything and stared at the screen. I wanted to apologize. But how could I if I couldn't say what I was apologizing for? *Sorry I'm dead now?*

I put my phone away.

The next day I lurched out to the bus stop still thinking about Nikki.

*Is it possible to keep a secret this big and still be best friends?* I wondered.

I didn't know if Nikki could handle dead me. But I knew I couldn't handle life without her. I had to do *something* to try to save our friendship.

I rounded the corner, hoping to see Nikki's blond hair and the denim jacket she always wore. The one we'd both sewn patches onto. Nikki was almost always at the bus stop before me. She wasn't there today.

I paced back and forth by the kerb and looked in the direction of Nikki's house. Finally I spotted Nikki's mum's red car and my friend's blond head in the back seat. I raised a hand to wave, but Nikki didn't even turn her head to look at me. They drove right past.

Going on the bus without my BFF was even worse the second time.

At school it was the same. I tried to catch up to Nikki. But it was useless.

Thanks to the embalming smoothie I had for breakfast, I was smelling a lot better. But throughout the day I felt more like a zombie than ever before. I staggered through the corridors and fumbled my way through lessons. Angela covered for me in biology. She did all the work while I moped.

"Are you worried about the kiss today?" Angela asked while she filled in our lab sheet.

"A bit," I said. I felt strange talking to Angela about Jeremy. It was weird talking to anybody but Nikki about my first kiss.

"I brought you this," Angela said.
She took out a tiny bottle of greenish liquid.
"It's a formaldehyde refresher. So you'll
know for certain that you smell OK. Maybe
a bit like coleslaw, but totally acceptable."

I tried to smile as I took the bottle.
Angela was being super nice. She was
amazing and had saved me more than
once. But she still wasn't Nikki.

# CHAPTER 8

I walked into the hall just in time to hear Ms Raimi, the dance teacher. She was going to lead the warm-ups.

"Come on, everyone!" Ms Raimi chirped. "Nothing like a little yoga to get the blood flowing and restore balance!"

"Ha! Yeah right," I muttered.

Nothing was ever going to get my blood flowing. And yoga sounded like a great way to tie myself up in knots. I backed out of the hall as quietly as possible. I lurched towards the toilets.

I went into a cubicle, leaned against the door and pulled out my phone. It was an old habit to check for messages from Nikki. But there were zero.

I sighed and put my head back. It was quiet and cool in the toilets. It felt nice. I was only planning to sit out warm-ups, but . . . *Maybe I'll stay here for the entire rehearsal*, I thought.

Even with my smelly issue taken care of, being in the musical wasn't fun anymore. Without Nikki, nothing was.

Suddenly the door banged opened. "Come on out, Tulah," a voice said.

I peaked through the crack in the door. Angela was standing in front of the sinks.

"Did you think I wouldn't notice that you were missing?" she said. "Honestly, the kiss won't be that bad. You'll survive . . . or whatever. It's technical rehearsal today anyway. Hammer might not even get to the scene with all the lighting and sound stuff we have to set up."

I was silent for a moment. "It's not just the kiss. It's this thing with Nikki," I confessed. "It makes me feel so horrible. I mean, we're finally onstage together sharing the spotlight, but we're not sharing anything else. It's all wrong. You know?"

"Not really," Angela admitted. "I've never had a friend like that. You two are lucky."

My new, tough-as-nails friend sounded kind of sappy. But I realized she was right. Nikki and I *were* lucky. Even if I never had a BFF like her again, we'd been each other's besties for years. Not everybody got that.

I peeked through the crack again. Sensitive Angela had disappeared, and Stage Manager Angela was back with her arms crossed over her chest. Her big black boots were planted in a wide stance.

"Now let's go, Tulah," she ordered. "Lucky or not, you know what they say. The show must go on!"

I sighed. "Fine." I opened the door and followed Angela back to the hall.

One of my Dad's favourite eye-rollers is the saying: *Whatever doesn't kill you makes you stronger.* I wasn't sure it still applied to me. I mean, technically I had already been knocked off by a zombie virus. But I hoped I could still become stronger from all this drama.

I stayed in the dark stage wings with Angela as much as possible. The main stage was busy with people adjusting the lights and shifting around scenery and microphones.

When Nikki got called up, I couldn't help but stare. The scowl never left her face as she took her marks. I hated that I'd made her so mad.

But then I noticed something. Nikki wasn't just frowning and glaring.

I nudged Angela. "Look! She's chewing her nail!" I whispered.

Angela gave me a funny look. "Lots of people do. Did you know we do manicures on the bodies that come into the funeral home? Your nails keep growing after you die."

I didn't know. Right now, I didn't care.

"Nikki only chews her nails when she feels sad!" I hissed.

Not mad. *Sad.*

Nikki wasn't sad very often. (Her nails usually looked great.) But when she thought about her Gran? She chewed her nail. When she was missing her cat Butterbean who disappeared last year? She chewed.

Somehow I knew Nikki wasn't thinking about Butterbean or Gran. Nikki was chomping on her nail because she was missing *me.* Just like I was missing her. Nikki had lost her best friend too, and she didn't even understand why.

At this point, old Tulah would've started leaking snot and salt water out of her face. I guess the new dead me couldn't make tears. But I really wished I could. The feelings I was having felt like they might boil over.

I looked up into the rafters because looking at Nikki was unbearable. My BFF was sad, and I wasn't there for her. *I* had abandoned *her.*

Overhead, I could see all the techs working. They were climbing around in the riggings and moving the lights so they would shine just right. A big guy in overalls leaned off the catwalk to move a heavy spotlight.

He kept one hand on the railing and stretched out the other one. He grabbed the light and pulled it closer. Then he started to undo the safety clasp.

It looked dangerous. If my stomach still did flips, it would've been doing cartwheels.

"Umm, Angela?" I glanced around, but she had left to help some people moving microphones.

I looked back up, hoping someone else had come to lend the tech a hand.

But it was too late.

The tech lost his grip. The light swung on its bar. As it swayed back and forth, I could tell it was going to fall from the rigging . . . right onto my best friend!

# CHAPTER 9

The light rolled off me, and I rolled off Nikki. We both struggled to get to our feet in a pool of broken glass.

"Are you OK?!" we asked each other at the same time.

I looked Nikki up and down. Even on stiff legs, I'd managed to get between her and the heavy spotlight that could've crushed her. She looked a tiny bit squashed (I had thrown myself on top of her, after all), but completely alive.

Except her face. Her mouth was hanging open. Her eyes were as big as volleyballs. All her colour had drained away.

For a split second, I thought maybe Nikki had turned into a zombie too. Only she had done it without any of the vomiting or dying or reanimating parts.

But then she pointed at me, and I looked down.

The spotlight had crashed into my right side. My clothes were a little torn up. (No big.) There was no blood. (Of course.) But my right arm was kind of dangling off at the elbow. Even though my arm didn't hurt, it *looked* super painful . . . and pretty gnarly.

Nikki could not stop staring.

Meanwhile, all around us, people were screaming and yelling and moving fast.

"Clear the stage!" someone yelled.

"Is everybody all right? What happened?" another person called.

Mr Hammer and Ms Raimi were yelling loudest. They sounded panicked.

I felt frozen. I knew I needed to hide my arm. I needed to tell Nikki something. Only I couldn't move!

Luckily *somebody* was still able to think on her feet.

A dark figure ran in from the side of the stage. It was Angela!

She put one arm around my shoulder. With the other she grabbed Nikki, who had been stuck in place with shock.

"You heard them! Clear the stage!" Angela shouted.

She pulled us both off the stage and through the curtained wings. We were moving before the teachers could see or say anything.

Angela pushed through the crowd of panicked kids. She didn't stop until we got to the greenroom and had shoved Nikki and me inside. She closed the door, spun around and leaned against it.

Angela took a second to recover her breath. Then she came over to take a look at my dangling arm.

That girl was all business.

I took a deep breath. Then I told Nikki everything. I told her about the eating raw flesh, the not sleeping, the stiffness, the embalming smoothies. EVERYTHING.

"The vomiting was the worst," I said. "No, the raw meat is the worst. No, no! Rotting is the worst!"

I paused and looked at Nikki. She just stared silently. But at least she was still standing there.

"Actually, the worst thing was keeping secrets from you," I said. "I was afraid that once you knew what I am, you'd run away screaming. I thought you'd be grossed out. I thought you wouldn't like me anymore."

Nikki cringed as she watched Angela pull a needle through my skin and tug the stitch tight. "This is all a little gross," she admitted.

Then she looked me in the eyes. "But I would never run away from you, Tulah. You're my best friend. We're friends for life."

Nikki came over and hugged my good side. "And afterlife!" she added with a grin.

I smiled too and squeezed back with one arm. "BFFs back in action!"

For a second it felt like everything was A-OK. Then Nikki pulled away. "Wait, so why did you tell Angela all this undead stuff?" she asked. Her smile was gone. "She was basically a complete stranger, but you trusted her more than me?"

"Tulah didn't tell me. I guessed," Angela said matter-of-factly as she tied off the last stitch. "I'm pretty familiar with dead people."

"But you two are the only ones who know," I said. "You two and Jaybee."

"Jaybee?" Nikki scowled harder. "You told *Jaybee* before me?"

"Not exactly. He worked it out too," I said. "I'm not very good at this whole zombie thing."

Angela looked up from packing her gear and raised an eyebrow. "Tell me about it."

"OMG," I told Nikki. "You should've seen me a couple of days ago."

"Or smelled her," Angela added.

"Wait. So that smell in my mum's car? That vomit-worthy, overcooked broccoli, grimy toilet smell? That was *you*?" Nikki asked. She smiled. I could tell she was trying hold back a chuckle, but it was hopeless.

Nikki burst into a fit of laughter. Then Angela laughed too. Then even I had to admit it was kind of hilarious. I doubled over laughing and almost smacked my head on a chair.

"Hey, careful," Angela said. "I just finished putting you back together."

# CHAPTER 10

The intercom in the greenroom crackled, interrupting our gut-busting giggle fest.

"Cast and crew of *Musical High,* please report to the hall!" the voice said.

The three of us made our way back and found seats near the stage. I sat cozy in the middle of my newest and oldest friends. I was so relieved to have come clean with Nikki (and even more relieved she still wanted to be friends). I felt practically normal.

"Sorry about that, everyone. We'll finish our tech rehearsal at a later date, after a formal safety review," Mr Hammer said. "Since we can't delay our opening, we don't have time to waste. So let's take it from the reunion scene. Tulah? Jeremy? You're on!"

I looked from Nikki to Angela and back. I didn't have to say a word. That was the thing about great friends. They knew exactly what I was thinking and feeling and not feeling.

"Time to pucker up, buttercup!" Nikki teased. She dug into her backpack and pulled out a roll of mints. "Here."

I covered my mouth. "Oh no. Do I stink?"

"I am getting a whiff of salt and vinegar chips," Nikki said. "This will take care of it. We can't have you kissing Jeremy with anything less than minty fresh breath."

I smiled and took two mints. "Thanks for having my back, bestie."

"OK, now go. And try not to break any more limbs," Angela added.

I carefully walked to the stage. I could feel Jeremy's eyes on me as I climbed the stairs.

Mr Hammer started us at the beginning of the scene. I managed to say my lines. But I wasn't sure how, because all I could think about was the fact that my lips were about to meet Jeremy Romero's!

With my zombie odour handled, I suddenly realized all the *normal* things that could go wrong with a kiss. It sounded easy, but what if my kiss was too hard? Or too soft? Or too wet? Or too dry? What if it was just too dead?

"There's something I wanted to give you . . ." I heard Jeremy's voice like it was coming from far away.

Suddenly it was time. Jeremy's face was right there.

His eyes were closing.

I leaned in.

We were kissing! We were actually kissing! And neither one of us was running away. I felt a shock, like the same little jolt I'd felt when I had got the part.

Then it was over. Jeremy stepped back. He smiled. I smiled too. I felt relieved and fizzy. The music to our duet swelled, but we both forgot to sing.

Out in the audience, I could hear Nikki cheering. A chorus of hoots and giggles rose up from the other cast members.

"All right, all right!" called Mr Hammer, trying to quiet everyone down.

"See? We got this," Jeremy said, just to me. He nudged me with his shoulder and flashed a shy smile.

I nudged back and grinned at my shoes.

"Good job, guys," Mr Hammer called up to us. "Let's keep it going. Forget about them," he added, waving at the audience.

I looked into Jeremy's deep brown eyes. The intro music began again, and I sang with all the passion in my undead heart.

Forgetting about the howling audience was easy.

Forgetting about the *kiss*? That wouldn't happen in a million years.

"Admit it, you two have been practising on your own!" Nikki whispered when I came off the stage on opening night.

I grinned. The kiss, under the lights and with the whole audience watching, was just as good as the first time. It didn't really take much acting on my part!

I glanced behind me to make sure Jeremy hadn't heard Nikki as he followed me offstage. But it was cool. Jeremy had stopped next to the curtain and was busy getting teased by his own friends.

"Nope. Only at rehearsals," I whispered back to Nikki. "There's no way I could keep *that* a secret."

"Looking good out there, you two," said a voice in the dark.

Angela walked out of the shadows and into the soft glow of the backstage light.

"Hey, we couldn't do it without you, Ms Stage Manager!" Nikki said.

Ever since my confession, Nikki and Angela had been getting along pretty well. It was a change to go from a duo to a trio, but I couldn't survive my death without *both* of them.

And Nikki was right. Angela was the best stage manager. People had no idea the work that goes on backstage. I barely noticed the change in music and lighting, but Angela didn't miss a beat.

"That's your cue," she told Nikki.

Nikki smiled and stepped onstage right on time. Soon the audience was roaring with laughter. Nikki was a natural. Jeremy and I might have been playing the leads, but Nikki stole the show.

I peeked through a crack in the set. I saw my parents and Jaybee in the audience. Of course my brother was reading a comic, but Mum and Dad were laughing and clapping with everyone else. I never thought I'd see this day – with me onstage, when the lights were up. Let alone in a leading role!

Sure, it might've taken being a zombie to kill my stage fright. That certainly had complications. But with my smoothies and mints and the help of my "expert team", I felt like I was finally working things out. And *that* felt fantastic.

Before I knew it, it was almost time for the finale.

"This has been the absolute best night of my life . . . I mean, death!" I whispered to Nikki and Angela.

Angela smirked. Nikki giggled.

"Remember to be careful out there," Angela said. Her smile disappeared. "There's not enough time to stitch you up before the curtain if you lose a limb."

"Yeah, *don't* break a leg," Nikki added.

"I promise," I told them, laughing. I held up my hand. "Pinky swear."

# TULAH'S TERMS

**blocking** planning out actors' movements onstage during a scene. So basically, Mr Hammer (our director) gets to be bossy and tell people where they should be and when.

**choreography** planned out dance moves. Choreography and stiff zombie limbs do not mix.

**corpse** simply put, a dead body

**decay** when stuff slowly breaks down and rots. Have you ever seen an old apple turn all wrinkly and brown and slimy? Yeah, that's decay, and it smells SUPER bad.

**embalming fluid** like Angela said, this is special liquid used to stop dead things from rotting. Formaldehyde is one kind. If a living person drank this stuff, it'd kill them. Good thing I'm already dead.

**flesh** soft parts of a person or animal . . . like the parts I want to eat

**formaldehyde** gas that when dissolved in water makes the perfect mixture to stop almost anything dead from rotting. It's really helpful for smelly zombies.

**funeral home** place where dead people are prepared for burial or cremation. Also the place where I can get patched up!

**greenroom** room backstage where people can hang out before or after they perform. The rooms aren't always green, which is kind of confusing, TBH.

**impulse** major, sudden desire to do something. You don't even think about it. You just do it.

**morgue** place where dead bodies are kept for a short time. Creepy.

**reanimate** bring back to life. I'm still trying to work out how it worked for me!

**rigging** equipment that holds up lights, curtains and more above a stage. There's lots of safety stuff to keep things in place, but sometimes people make mistakes. . .

**rigor mortis** when the muscles and joints in a dead body get all stiff. It starts a few hours after death and lasts a few days (at least for normal people).

**stench** seriously nasty smell

**wings** parts of a stage that the audience can't see. In other words, the safest spot for chickens like the alive me.

**zombie apocalypse** when a load of zombies rise up and attack the living. It's worse than the middle school mean girls' rude attitudes at lunch, but just barely.

# USE YOUR BRAAAAINS!

Don't worry, I won't eat them.

Tulah, that was great! Want to run it again? Tulah? Tulah?!

Pssst, Tulah! Look, my dad got free makeup samples!

1. I totally missed the fact that Nikki was upset with me. Help me out, and let me know how you think she feels here. If you want to be an overachiever, go back to page 25 and tell that weekend from Nikki's point of view.

Maybe too well . . .

PO.

2. What are the tiny lines swirling all around me on page 48? What makes you think that? Try coming up with some other ways to draw the same effect.

3. The big CREEK! is called a sound effect. They help show and describe sounds in comics. What do you think is making that scary sound? (Flip back to page 88 if you need help.) What's about to happen?

CREEEEEEK!

4. Nikki knows my undead secret. Now I'm starting to wonder if I should tell my parents too. Is that a good idea or totally insane? Write what you think, and make sure you give lots of reasons for whatever you choose – I need a strong argument!

5. My BFF and I eventually got through our rotten drama. But maybe I could've handled things differently with Nikki. Do you have any advice for me? How have you solved your friendship problems?

6. OMG. My pinkie popped off right before the big finale! Where did it go?! Can I find it, or hide my hand so no one notices? Will I be exposed? If you're dying to know what happens next, try writing your own ending to my undead tale.

## OMG, ZOMBIE!

After eating a suspicious school meal, I feel different. REALLY different. Find out how my undead life began!

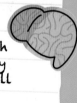

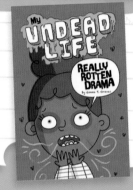

## REALLY ROTTEN DRAMA

I'm dealing with a BFF crisis, my first-ever (stage) kiss and my rotting zombie body! Can I put an end to this stinky situation?

## TOTAL FREAK-OUT

No meat equals one grumpy zombie. Can I get enough food to keep my mood under control before the school dance?

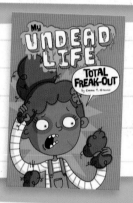

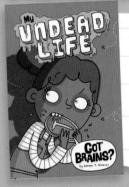

## GOT BRAINS?

I'm going on a retreat with the academic team (and my nemesis, Bella Gulosi!). Will I survive the weekend?

## About the Author

Emma T. Graves has written more than ninety books for children and has written about characters both living and dead. When she's not writing, Emma enjoys watching classic horror films, taking long walks in the nearby cemetery and storing up food in her cellar. She is prepared for the zombie apocalypse.

## About the Illustrator

Binny Boo, otherwise known as Ellie O'Shea, is a coffee addict, avid snowboarder, puppy fanatic – and an illustrator. Her love for art started at a young age. She spent her childhood drawing, watching cartoons, creating stories and eating too many sweets for her own good. She graduated from Plymouth University in 2015 with a degree in illustration. She now lives in Worcester and feels so lucky that she gets to spend her days doing what she adores.